W9-BHR-156
DISCARD

Chicken Chickens Go to School

Valeri Gorbachev

A CHESHIRE STUDIO BOOK

North-South Books · New York · London

One fine day, Mother Hen took her two little chickens to school for the very first time.

The little chickens were a little scared.
"Don't worry," said Mother Hen as she waved good-bye,
"I'm sure you will like it here."

"Hello," said Mrs. Heron the teacher, "welcome to my class."
"We're scared," said the chickens. "We don't know anyone."
"Don't worry," said Mrs. Heron. "I'm sure you will make friends quickly."

1 2 3

1 2 3

"Can we make friends with anyone in the class?" asked the chickens.

Mrs. Heron smiled. "Of course you can," she said.

During playtime, all the chickens could think about was making friends.

Beaver is very big, they thought. It would be good to have her as a friend. So they walked up to Beaver and said hello.

"Sssssssh," said Beaver, "I'm trying to build this tower!"

During story time, the chickens sat next to Rabbit. Rabbit looks friendly, they thought. He would be a good friend. So they turned to Rabbit and said hello.

"Sssssssh," said Rabbit, "I'm listening to the story."

During music time the chickens stood next to Frog. Frog is little just like us, thought the chickens. Maybe he would be our friend. So the chickens turned to Frog and said hello.

"Sssssssh," said Frog, "I'm trying to sing."

During snack time the two little chickens sat all by themselves.
No one wants to make friends with us, they thought.

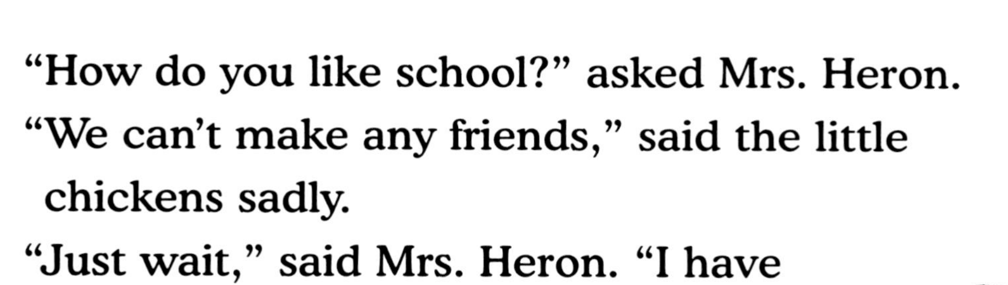

"How do you like school?" asked Mrs. Heron.
"We can't make any friends," said the little chickens sadly.
"Just wait," said Mrs. Heron. "I have a feeling you will."

After everyone cleaned up, it was time to go outside.
"Come along," said Mrs. Heron. "We'll go to the meadow."
The whole class cheered.

On the way, everyone crossed a little stream.
Everyone except the little chickens.

“What’s wrong?” asked Mrs. Heron.
“We’re too little,” said the chickens. “We might fall off the rocks—and we can’t swim!”
“Don’t be such chicken chickens,” said Beaver. “The water isn’t very deep. You can do it.”
“No,” they said. “We’re just little chickens.”

"I could build a bridge over the water," said Beaver.

"I could leap across the stream
carrying the chickens,"
said Rabbit.

"I could teach the chickens how to swim," said Frog.

"Thank you all," said Mrs. Heron, "but I have a better idea. Why don't you hold hands with the chickens and help them over the rocks?"

So they all held hands and slowly crossed the stream.

"We did it!" cried the little chickens. "Thank you for helping us."

The little chickens had a wonderful time playing in the meadow with their new friends.

On the way back to school, the little chickens scampered across the rocks all by themselves. "Hurray for the little chickens!" everyone cried.

After school Mother Hen was waiting. "Goodness," she said as the little chickens ran down the stairs. "You both look very happy."

"We *like* school," they said. "We made lots of friends."

"That's wonderful," said Mother Hen.

As the little chickens headed home they turned and waved.

"Good-bye, friends," they called, "see you tomorrow!"

For Didier

A CHESHIRE STUDIO BOOK
First published in the United States, Great Britain, Canada, Australia, and New Zealand in 2003 by North-South Books, an imprint of Nord-Süd Verlag AG, Gossau Zürich, Switzerland. Distributed in the United States by North-South Books Inc., New York.
Library of Congress Cataloging-in-Publication Data is available.
The CIP catalogue record for this book is available from The British Library.
ISBN 0-7358-1600-X (trade edition)
1 3 5 7 9 HC 10 8 6 4 2
ISBN 0-7358-1767-7 (library edition)
1 3 5 7 9 LE 10 8 6 4 2
Printed in Italy